The Lion AND THE Mouse

Dona Herweck Rice

Editorial Director
Dona Herweck Rice

Assistant Editor
Leslie Huber, M.A.

Editor-in-Chief
Sharon Coan, M.S.Ed.

Editorial Manager
Gisela Lee, M.A.

Creative Director
Lee Aucoin

Illustration Manager/Designer
Timothy J. Bradley

Illustrator
Karen Lowe

Publisher
Rachelle Cracchiolo, M.S.Ed.

Teacher Created Materials
5301 Oceanus Drive
Huntington Beach, CA 92649-1030
http://www.tcmpub.com
ISBN 978-1-4333-0293-0
©2009 Teacher Created Materials, Inc.
Printed in China
Nordica.072018.CA21800844

The Lion and the Mouse

Story Summary

While a mighty lion sleeps, a small mouse runs up its back and gets tangled in its mane. The lion is angry. No one should disturb the king of the beasts! The lion says that it will eat the mouse. But the mouse pleads for its life. The mouse claims that one day it may be able to save the life of the lion. The lion laughs at that. How could a tiny mouse save a mighty lion? But the lion decides to free the mouse anyway.

Later, the lion is caught in a hunter's net. The lion cannot escape. Can the mouse save the lion from the hunter's trap? Read the story and you will find out.

Tips for Performing Reader's Theater

Adapted from Aaron Shepard

- Don't let your script hide your face. If you can't see the audience, your script is too high.

- Look up often when you speak. Don't just look at your script.

- Talk slowly, so the audience knows what you are saying.

- Talk loudly, so everyone can hear you.

- Talk with feelings. If the character is sad, let your voice be sad. If the character is surprised, let your voice be surprised.

- Stand up straight. Keep your hands and feet still.

- Remember that even when you are not talking, you are still your character.

- Narrator, be sure to give the characters enough time for their lines.

Tips for Performing Reader's Theater *(cont.)*

- If the audience laughs, wait for them to stop before you speak again.

- If someone in the audience talks, don't pay attention.

- If someone walks into the room, don't pay attention.

- If you make a mistake, pretend it was right.

- If you drop something, try to leave it where it is until the audience is looking somewhere else.

- If a reader forgets to read his or her part, see if you can read the part instead, make something up, or just skip over it. Don't whisper to the reader!

- If a reader falls down during the performance, pretend it didn't happen.

The Lion and the Mouse

Characters

Narrator	Leopard
Lion	Cuckoo
Mouse	Hunter

Setting

This reader's theater takes place in a thick, green jungle. The sounds of animals fill the hot and humid air. The den of a mighty lion can be found deep in the heart of this jungle.

Act 1

Narrator:	Come with me deep in the jungle. There is a cave covered in vines. The air is moist and heavy. The sounds of jungle animals can be heard. Monkeys chatter and parrots call. Outside the cave, the King of Beasts slowly raises its shaggy head and . . .
Lion:	Roar!
Narrator:	The lion is grumpy. The animal chatter has wakened it from a deep sleep.
Lion:	Who disturbs my sleep? Come forward if you dare!
Narrator:	Nobody stirs.
Leopard:	Who are you kidding, old buddy? No one is brave enough to admit to waking you. You'd eat the poor creature for breakfast!

Narrator:	The leopard is the lion's oldest friend. It is the only one who can get away with this kind of talk.
Lion:	Yawn! Well, anyone who wakes me up deserves to be eaten for breakfast.
Leopard:	Boy, sometimes it's not so easy being your friend! You sure are lucky that I'm still around.
Lion:	Me, lucky? You get to be friends with the King of Beasts. You're the lucky one.
Narrator:	The lion and leopard argue a great deal. They do not always seem like friends.
Lion:	Now, go away. I need my beauty sleep.
Leopard:	Aye, aye, your majesty! Your wish is my command.

Narrator:	The leopard leaps off into the jungle. The lion yawns again. Then the lion lowers its heavy head and falls back to sleep.
Lion:	Zzzz.

Act 2

Narrator:	There is a sudden rustle nearby. A tiny gray mouse appears from beneath a vine.
Mouse:	Now where is that old bird?
Narrator:	The mouse is looking for its friend, the cuckoo bird.
Mouse:	Maybe if I climb this little hill, I'll get a better look. Cuckoo! Cuckoo!
Narrator:	The mouse doesn't see that the "hill" is really the lion's furry back.

Mouse:	What a soft and cozy hill this is! But what's all this fur doing on top of a hill?
Narrator:	The mouse is now in the lion's furry mane.
Mouse:	Cuckoo! Cuckoo! Where are you? I can't see anything through this fur!
Narrator:	The mouse stops suddenly.
Mouse:	Wait a minute! This is no hill! Oh, no! I'm trapped in all this fur. Help!
Narrator:	The lion wakes with a start.
Lion:	What? What's going on here? Roar!
Mouse:	Help me! Help me!
Narrator:	With its sharp claws, the lion lifts the mouse by the tail. It dangles the mouse in front of its face.

Mouse:	Squeak.
Lion:	Is that all you have to say for yourself?
Mouse:	Excuse me. I didn't mean to disturb you.
Lion:	I should think not.
Mouse:	I was just looking for my friend, the cuckoo. I thought you were a small hill.
Lion:	A hill?
Mouse:	Yes, a hill. I forgot that hills don't have fur.
Lion:	You forgot, did you?
Mouse:	I am sorry. Truly I am. But if you will just put me down, I will be on my way. I won't disturb you again.

Lion: You are right. You won't disturb me. Because I will eat you now.

Mouse: Gulp. Oh, you do not want to do that. I am a very little bite, as you can see. And who knows? One day I may be of great help to you.

Lion: What a laugh! You help me? Impossible!

Mouse: I beg your pardon. But it is possible. You might be surprised.

Lion: Ha! You are wrong, little mouse. But you do make me laugh.

Mouse: I didn't mean to be funny. But if you like me, I'm glad of it.

Lion: I am going to let you go. But I warn you. I won't be so kind another time.

Mouse: Oh, thank you, thank you. You won't be sorry. Just wait and see!

Narrator: The lion lowers its big paw to the ground and lets the mouse run free. The mouse scampers away. As it nears the safety of the trees, the mouse turns and speaks.

Mouse: I will help you one day. I promise I will. You are now my true friend. I am your true friend, too. You have my word.

Poem: The Arrow and the Song

Act 3

Narrator: Back in the trees, the mouse finds the cuckoo right away.

Cuckoo: Coo-coo! Coo-coo!

Mouse: There you are! Where have you been?

Cuckoo: I was above you in the trees and saw the whole thing. I was afraid for you, but I didn't know what to do!

Mouse: Don't worry. The lion is my friend now.

Cuckoo: You are my friend, and I like you, but you are cuckoo if you think the lion is your friend. That lion eats mice like you for breakfast!

Mouse: Don't be so quick to judge the lion.

Cuckoo: I will try not to, but promise me you will be safe. Do not go near the lion again.

Mouse: Don't worry, friend! I will be all right.

Narrator: Back at the lion's den, the leopard has returned.

Leopard: I can't believe what I just saw! That mouse woke you up, and you let it go! Now I've seen it all.

Lion: Maybe I'm not as grumpy as you think.

Leopard: That's a laugh! You're the biggest grump in the jungle. They should probably call you the King of Grumps.

Lion: You better watch out, or I may eat you for breakfast!

Leopard: Ha! You can't fool me, you old softy.

Lion: Oh, go away and let me go back to sleep.

Leopard: I think I'll take a little nap myself, now that you mention it. Sweet dreams, old pal of mine.

Lion: Zzzz.

Act 4

Narrator: The sleeping animals don't know there is danger nearby. A hunter quietly creeps through the trees.

Hunter: Ah, this looks like an excellent place to set my trap.

Narrator: The hunter does not speak but instead thinks these words.

Hunter: I must be very quiet so that the animals are unaware that I'm here.

Narrator: The hunter carries a large net made of sturdy rope.

Hunter: This is a perfect spot! I will spread the net here on the ground, and then I will tie this rope to the tree above it.

Narrator:	The hunter works quickly and with skill.
Hunter:	When a large animal steps into this net, the rope will pull it up with the animal inside. When I return to check, I will bring my spear and kill whatever is in the trap. It will not be able to escape.
Narrator:	The hunter does not see the cuckoo bird in the tree above.
Cuckoo:	I must warn the animals to stay away! Coo-coo! Coo-coo!
Narrator:	The cuckoo flies swiftly through the jungle to warn everyone. All the animals listen. But the lion is fast asleep and does not hear.

Hunter: I wonder which animal will be caught in my trap. Maybe I will be lucky and catch the King of Beasts! Its fur is precious and will make me rich!

Lion: Zzzz.

Act 5

Narrator: After a long sleep, the lion wakes at last.

Lion: I am feeling very hungry now. I'll just look around for a bite to eat.

Narrator: The lion steps from its den. But it steps right into the hunter's net!

Lion: Roar! What's this?

Narrator: From across the jungle, the hunter hears the roar.

Hunter: Can it be? Have I caught the King of Beasts? I'm on my way!

Lion: I'm trapped! I can't get out of this net. The rope is strong. What can I do? Roar! Roar!

Narrator: Someone else hears the lion. It is the mouse.

Mouse: I am coming, friend!

Narrator: The mouse finds the lion fast. The lion hangs from a tree in the net. The cuckoo and leopard watch, but they don't know what to do.

Lion: I am trapped. I can't get out!

Mouse: But I can help!

Lion: How?

Mouse: Watch!

Narrator: The mouse climbs the tree and down the rope. It uses its strong teeth to gnaw at the rope. Snip, snap! The rope breaks and the net drops to the ground. The lion is free!

Cuckoo and Leopard: Hooray!

Lion: Thank you, little mouse! You have saved me. You truly are my friend.

Mouse: I only did for you what you did for me. And I was glad to do it.

Lion: You taught me an important lesson. Even the small and weak may be of help to the large and powerful. Today a small mouse proved to be more powerful than the King of Beasts. Let's have a cheer for the hero of the day!

All: Hip-hip-hooray! Hip-hip-hooray! Hip-hip hooray!

Song: When Johnny Comes Marching Home

The Arrow and the Song
by Henry Wadsworth Longfellow

I shot an arrow into the air,
It fell to earth, I knew not where;
For, so swiftly it flew, the sight
Could not follow it in its flight.

I breathed a song into the air,
It fell to earth, I knew not where;
For who has sight so keen and strong,
That it can follow the flight of song?

Long, long afterward, in an oak
I found the arrow, still unbroke;
And the song, from beginning to end,
I found again in the heart of a friend.

When Johnny Comes Marching Home
Traditional

When Johnny comes marching home again,
Hurrah! Hurrah!
We'll give him a hearty welcome then,
Hurrah! Hurrah!
The men will cheer and the boys will shout,
The ladies they will all turn out,
And we'll shout, "Hooray!"
When Johnny comes marching home.

The old church bell will peal with joy,
Hurrah! Hurrah!
To welcome home our darling boy,
Hurrah! Hurrah!
The village lads and lassies say
With roses they will strew the way,
And we'll shout, "Hooray!"
When Johnny comes marching home.

Get ready for the Jubilee,
Hurrah! Hurrah!
We'll give the hero three times three,
Hurrah! Hurrah!
The laurel wreath is ready now
To place upon his loyal brow,
And we'll shout, "Hooray!"
When Johnny comes marching home.

Glossary

aye — yes

cuckoo — a grayish bird whose call sounds like its name

humid — moist

impossible — not able to happen

jubilee — party; celebration

laurel wreath — crown of leaves that is placed on the head of a hero or a winner of a competition

leopard — a large spotted animal in the cat family

mane — the long hair growing on or around the back or neck of an animal

peal — ringing sound

rustle — a group of slight, soft sounds

scampers — runs quickly and lightly

shaggy — covered with long untidy hair

strew — cover or sprinkle over

swiftly — quickly